Molly and The Cat Who Stole Her Tongue

BY LUCY BELL
Illustrated by Linda D. Martin

To Phyllis,
    Carol and I have been friends for more than 70 years.
    Many of the scenes in this book are from our childhood home town.
    I hope Kaela Li will like this book someday. :)

Lucy Bell

AMBIENT LIGHT PUBLISHERS

Ambient Light Publishers, LLC
PO Box 9105
Colorado Springs, CO 80932

Publisher's Cataloging-in-Publication data

Bell, Lucy, 1941-
    Molly and the cat who stole her tongue / Lucy Bell ; illustrated
    by Linda D. Martin
    p. cm.
    ISBN 978-0-9863324-3-2 (pbk.)
            978-0-9863324-4-9 (ebook)
    1. Bell, Lucy, 1941- 2. Martin, Linda D., 1961-, ill. 3. Juvenile
Fiction - Readers - Chapter Books 4. Juvenile Fiction - Animals
General 5. Juvenile Fiction - Historical - United States - 20th
Century 6. Juvenile Fiction - Historical - United States - North
Dakota 7. Juvenile Fiction - Social Themes - Self-Esteem & Self-
Reliance 8. Juvenile Fiction - Social Themes - Bullying
    PZ7.1.B455 Mo 2016
    813.'6

                                                        2016946894

For all the brave children in the world

TABLE OF CONTENTS

CHAPTER 1

MOLLY GETS A PRESENT

Molly walked through the overgrown chokecherry bushes until she came to her favorite tree—the spreading cottonwood she called Kathleen after her mother. Molly climbed onto the friendly low branch. It felt like a mother's lap. She was only four when the accident happened, but she remembered her mother's lap.

She leaned back, enjoying the green shady comfort of the O'Neill place. The smell of vegetable soup seeped from the leaning brick chimney of the ramshackle house, a sure sign that Mrs. O'Neill was making lunch for her old husband and herself. Beyond the house stood a sagging barn with faded posters from last year's county fair nailed to the boards.

Rustling grass made Molly turn to see two girls from her third grade class approaching. They stopped under the tree and looked up at Molly.

Pam shook her red curls. "So, Molly, how's your summer vacation going?"

Jamie stuck her hands into the pockets of her overalls. "Pam, why do you ask her a question? You know she can't talk. The cat stole her tongue."

The girls snickered at the teasing joke that Molly heard every day since she'd been the new girl at school, three months ago.

Pam put her hand over her mouth until she got control of herself. "Even if the cat … uh, uh, I mean, even if you can't talk, Jamie and I brought you a present. Get off that branch and we'll give it to you."

Molly wondered if they wanted to be friends. They weren't nice to her at school. They never picked her for hopscotch at recess, but a present would be exciting. She slid off the branch and retied the sash that had come loose on the waist of her faded blue cotton jumper.

Pam opened a brown paper bag. "Here, Jamie, you do it."

Jamie pulled a jar out of the bag, unscrewed the lid and dumped the contents onto the top of Molly's head.

"EEEK!" They both screamed and jumped backward.

"I don't believe it. She is not even screaming."

"You stupid girl. There is a big fat spider in your hair."

"Let's get out of here!" Jamie dropped the jar in the grass as they ran away.

Molly shook her chestnut braids, and the round, big-bodied yellow spider with orange and white striped legs dropped down in the grass by the jar. Molly had never seen one like it before.

She picked it up and put it back into the jar, leaving the lid loose. *Don't worry. I'll set you free. But first I want to show you to Uncle. He might know your name.*

Thanks. Stuffy in jar. Molly heard the spider's thoughts. She smiled at her new friend.

Molly looked across the street to Wilma's Filling Station where she lived with Aunt and Uncle in the back of the combination gas station and general store. She saw Bertha Olson's beat-up white Studebaker coupe parked by the gas pump. Molly didn't want to face Aunt Wilma and Bertha at the same time. They were like a grown up version of Pam and Jamie.

Molly walked as far as the barn and sat down. She gazed at the old posters. "Kelly Brothers Carnival Rides," "Gypsy Rosemary Fortune Telling," "Amazing Dr. Jenkins Cures Insomnia." Molly remembered Aunt talking about the last one. Mr. Jenkins wasn't a doctor at all, and the sheriff closed him down for being a fake.

Blackie, the O'Neill's old cat who'd lost a front paw years ago in a mouse trap, climbed onto Molly's lap, curling around the jar with the spider in it.

Molly spoke to them in her mind. *I always thought I could talk. I thought it was just the scared feeling that stopped me. I want to talk but the words won't come out. Maybe the kids are right. Maybe the Cat did steal my tongue.* Molly stuck out her

tongue and bit down on it. *I have a tongue. But it doesn't work. Somewhere there is a mean Cat who has stolen the talk right out of my tongue.*

CHAPTER 2

WILMA'S FILLING STATION

Molly glanced across the street and sighed. Bertha's car was still there. She lifted Blackie off her lap and stood up. Aunt would throw a fit if she showed up late for supper. Tucking the jar into the pocket of her jumper, she crossed the dusty street to the store.

"Here she is," Aunt said loudly, as Molly came in. "Never said a word all morning."

Standing behind the candy-counter, Aunt leaned forward, her elbows resting on the glass top. Inside the sliding doors candy bars beckoned—Baby Ruth in its red and white wrapper, 5th Avenue in gold letters, chocolate covered Cherry Bing. Next to them pastel colored Necco wafers and sugared jelly Chuckles lay in a row. One-cent Bazooka and Pal bubble gum shared the space with Chiclets, Black Jack and Cloves chewing gum, and paper packets of Sen-Sen breath freshener.

Molly saw that Frieda Schmidt had walked over from her waitress job on Main Street. Frieda shook the salty Planter's peanuts into her hand from the cellophane bag she'd just bought for a nickel. Bertha, sitting in the chair by the red Coca-Cola cooler, took another swallow from the green-glass coke bottle.

Aunt scowled down at Molly. "Our little town of Cando was named for its Can-Do spirit, and that means you talk, Molly. You hear me?"

She looked back at her friends. "She's been here three months. I told her from the beginning she darn well better speak up. Hmmph. Not one peep."

Frieda shook her head in disbelief. "How did you get her again, Wilma?"

Aunt folded her arms across her chest. "Train hit 'em. Unmarked crossing somewhere out in Ohio. She was four years old. Don't know how she survived, but she's been in foster homes for the last four years. Somebody connected the Goodwin name. Turned out her dad was Henry's long lost little brother."

Bertha gulped the last of her coke. "Maybe she takes after Henry. He doesn't exactly have the Gift of Gab."

The women went into a fit of laughter at this remark. Molly bit her lip, thinking of her quiet, gentle uncle.

"At least Henry says something, every great once in a while, not like. . ." She gave her chin a jerk in Molly's direction.

Frieda finished her peanuts. "Well, I feel for you. Lucky for her you took her in."

"You better believe it. She was so peculiar nobody kept her for very long."

Aunt frowned at Molly. "I don't know why you're standing gawking. Go get ready for supper."

Molly left the voices behind, and headed to her room, a former storage shed attached to Aunt and Uncle's small apartment in the back of the building.

Uncle wasn't home yet. He liked to get away with his books and studies. He had a portable blue Royal typewriter that he carried in a black case with a handle. Sometimes Molly saw him go to the post office with manila envelopes full of papers.

R-r-r-k! Plap! Molly heard the screen door close. Uncle was home for supper. Good. She wanted to show him the spider.

After they ate, Molly and Uncle did the dishes. Uncle lifted the pot from the top of the coal burning stove and poured the heated water into two blue metal dishpans on the kitchen counter. He added soap to one and swished it around with his hand making a layer of bubbles. He left the hot water in the other dishpan clear for rinsing.

Molly washed. Uncle rinsed, dried and put away.

Aunt sprawled on the couch in the living room listening to her program. Soon the radio voices of "One Man's Family" were drowned out by Aunt's snoring.

Molly brought the jar holding the spider to the kitchen table where Uncle sat reading a book about plants. He looked up.

"Looks like you've got something to show me. What's in your jar?"

Molly showed him.

"Well, I declare, it's a cat-face spider."

Uncle turned the jar so that the spider's abdomen was upside-down facing Molly. It looked just like a child's drawing of a cat's face! Two pointed ears, two eyes and a nose. Molly smiled. Her new friend was cute!

"This is a good spider, Molly. It doesn't harm people, and it eats insects that are harmful to plants. We often see them in early summer. You can keep it tonight and release it in the morning."

Tucked in bed, with Cat-Face in the jar on her nightstand, Molly sent her thoughts to the spider. *There are good Cats and bad Cats in this world. You are a good Cat. But the Cat who stole my tongue is a very bad Cat. What can I do? I want to talk!*

Find the Cat.

Molly sat up on her elbow and stared at the spider in the moonlight. *What did you say?*

I said find the Cat.

CHAPTER 3

RUSTY AND TONY

M olly woke up the next morning, glad that it was summer vacation. She turned the page on the Boy Scout calendar Uncle had hung on her wall. He told her a famous artist named Norman Rockwell had drawn the pictures. "June 1, 1950." She had three whole months before school started again.

Molly decided she'd walk down by the river today. She pictured the happy golden faces of the dandelions that would smile up at her. A voice interrupted her thoughts. *Help us. Get us out of here.*

Molly remembered the spider. Why would she say "us"?

She looked in the jar. Only one spider. Oh well. *Cat-Face. I remember my promise. I'll set you free this morning.*

Lilac bush.

You want to be let go under the lilac bush?

Lilac bush.

After breakfast, Molly went straight to the branchy lilac bush that stood by Uncle's wildflower garden. MMMM! Molly breathed the delicious fragrance of the blossoms. Before Molly set it down, Cat-Face jumped from the jar and scurried away.

Wait! Last night you told me to find the Cat. I don't know how to do that. Can't you help me?

But Cat-Face was gone.

Back inside Molly grabbed an apple, the book on sunflowers Uncle had given her, and skipped down to the river. She leaned against the trunk of a gnarled elm tree, and opened the book, but she couldn't concentrate. Cat-Face's words kept going through her mind. *Find the Cat.*

I know I need to find the Cat. But I can't do it by myself. I need help. I don't want to ask Uncle. He has enough trouble dealing with Aunt.

Molly took a bite of the apple and put it down beside her to turn the page. At that moment, a flying ball of reddish-brown fur zipped past her and snatched the apple. Then it stopped short and looked at her. Molly saw that the fast-moving thief was a wiggly cocker spaniel, who now held the apple between his paws. His tail wagged so hard his whole rear end shook.

Hey, you stole my apple! Molly thought, looking at the lively dog.

Oops. Sorry. The dog thought back. *I sort of ruined your apple. It would still be good for a game of catch. Want to play?*

Okay. Molly picked up the apple and threw it high and far. The little red dog took off like a shot, grabbed the apple before it landed, and came running back to her.

He dropped the apple at her feet. *Let's do it again.*

This time Molly ran with the dog, throwing the apple ahead of her, and catching up with him as he caught it. Molly threw the apple too far. It rolled down the bank into the river and bounced into the water.

I'm sorry, Molly said and then laughed. The dog had sprawled out flat on his stomach with his back legs straight out behind. He looked like a throw rug.

Molly knelt down in the grass. *My name is Molly. What's yours?*

I'm Rusty. Nice to meet you.

A movement caught Molly's eye and she turned to see a giant-sized Labrador retriever with wet fur and the apple in his mouth. He trotted over and dropped the apple. *Did somebody lose this?*

Rusty circled the newcomer. *We did, Tony. This is my new friend Molly. She can talk to us.*

Rusty ran off to chase a gray squirrel with a wide golden tail, who'd stolen the remains of the apple.

Tony lay down in the grass across from Molly. Except for white hair under his chin and the sides of his wide nose, his coat was completely black.

Do you live around here? Molly asked.

Rusty and I live in that cave in the riverbank. Tony looked toward an opening a few yards away.

You mean you don't have owners?

Tony looked down. *My person was old and she died. Her neighbor put me in the shelter, but I'm not young myself and nobody wanted to adopt me. Nobody wanted to adopt Rusty either. They said he was too hyper.*

I didn't know there was an animal shelter in Cando.

There isn't. We were in Rock Lake.

You see, Tony looked sideways at Rusty, still distracted by the squirrel. *I was beginning to think our days were numbered. When a new volunteer took us for a walk, we saw our chance and ran away. I knew we'd be picked up and put back in the shelter if we stayed in Rock Lake, so we kept following the river until we got here. I knew this town because my owner used to bring me here for my shots.*

Rusty heard the end of the conversation and joined them. *That's the day we met the vet.*

Tony explained. *Rusty cut the pad on his front paw on a tin can in the river. I took him to Dr. Wellman, the vet. Rusty ran into the waiting room. When he got back here he had stitches.*

Rusty turned his paw over to show Molly. *After it healed up, I chewed the stitches out myself. I didn't like the stitches, but I like Dr. Wellman.*

I know him, Molly said. *He talked to our class about pet care.*

Rusty wagged his tail. *Your turn, Molly. What brings you here?*

Molly thought of the spider's message. *I'm looking for a cat.*

A cat! Rusty jumped up and spun in a circle. *That's what I do all day long! Find cats and chase them. I don't want to catch one. I just like to chase the bejiggers out of them. I didn't know people like to do that, too.*

Molly laughed. *I don't want to chase a cat. I'm looking for a certain cat. It's a long story. Are you sure you want to hear it?*

Tony settled down in the grass. *Tell us.*

Rusty gave his long silky ears a shake, and sat down, still panting from the squirrel chase. *We're all ears.*

Molly told the two dogs everything that had happened. Tony raised his eyebrows. *So you think a cat stole your tongue? I've never heard of that before.*

Me either, Rusty added. *But it doesn't surprise me. I've never trusted cats.*

Maybe we can help you find the Cat, Tony said.

Cats talk to me, Rusty said. *They call me names when I chase them. FLAP-EARS, SLOBBER FACE, STINKY FUR-BALL.*

That's enough Rusty, we get the idea, Tony cautioned.

Molly looked thoughtful. *We need a plan. I have to go home now to help Aunt with chores. Let's think about it and I'll come back tomorrow.*

Molly left the dogs and stopped along the way to watch a yellow and black striped caterpillar in the grass when she heard the same voices she'd heard that morning. *Help us. We want to go home.*

CHAPTER 4

THE SECRET PLAN

Molly woke up the next morning eager to see her new friends, but her thoughts were interrupted by Aunt's voice.

"Molly, I need you to help me with the wash. Eat some toast and then come down to the basement."

Molly did as she was told and found Aunt by the round porcelain washing machine feeding the rinsed clothes into the wringer at the top.

Molly caught the flattened wet pieces and lowered them into the basket below. She put the clothespin bag on top and carried the load to the clothesline where she pinned them up to dry in the warm breeze.

Back in the house Aunt was on the phone. This would be a good time to go to the river.

Rusty ran to meet her, barking. *Good news! We finally found a cat that knows something.*

Tony joined them. *Let's say we have some information. Maybe you can figure out what to do with it.*

Molly sat down in the sunshine and crossed her legs.

Tony began. *I met a Siamese cat named Gloria. Her owners recently got her from the shelter in Rock Lake. I told her your story. She said Rock Lake has a lot of mean cats. She was homeless for a while and lived in alleys where she saw cats almost kill each other over a fish head.*

Rusty wrinkled his nose. *I don't like the head part, myself. I leave it. Eyeballs. Yuck!*

Never mind, Rusty. The point is Gloria said that it sounds like we are dealing with a mean cat, and Rock Lake is full of them. She's thankful she got adopted.

We need to go to Rock Lake. You walked from there. Is it far? Do you remember how to get there?

Rusty wagged his tail. *Easy as pie. We followed the river. It took us two days.*

Molly patted Rusty's head. *I want to give it a try. If only I can think of some way to get away without Aunt and Uncle stopping me.*

That night at supper, Aunt announced, "Uncle and I are going to Carrington to visit my sister tomorrow. It's a long drive, an hour past Rock Lake. We'll be gone all day. You may come along if you plan on talking to them. Otherwise, stay home. I don't want any Silent Susy-Q embarrassing me in front of my sister."

Molly took a bite of her chicken drumstick.

"Now, Wilma, the child is never any trouble. She might enjoy the trip. If she doesn't go, maybe I'll stay home, too."

Uncle passed the mashed potatoes to Molly.

"Henry Goodwin, you'll do no such thing. You know my lumbago has been acting up. I would never be able to drive that far by myself. I might even have to lie down in the back seat."

Molly finished drinking her milk. She looked into Uncle's concerned face and smiled to let him know she would be fine. At the same time the idea she'd been searching for popped up in her brain.

After Aunt and Uncle were asleep, Molly crept to Uncle's desk where she found paper and an ink-pen.

Her cursive wasn't very good and she had to write the note over and over to get it to look right.

Finally it was ready. It said:

Dear Mr. and Mrs. Goodwin,
I'm sorry you weren't home. I have missed Molly since she left. I've asked her to spend the weekend with me. I will bring her back early next week.
Alice Perkins (Molly's last foster parent.)

Molly tiptoed back to her room with the letter. She would leave it on the kitchen table the next morning after Aunt and Uncle left. Molly didn't like to tell fibs but she had to do it. If she found the Cat and came back talking, even Aunt would be happy.

The sun hadn't risen when Molly heard the old Ford crank up and back away. Gasoline fumes mixed with dust blew through her open window. Lucky that Aunt believed in getting an early start.

Molly packed her knapsack with sandwiches, apples, two soup bones, some cookies and a thermos of lemonade. She grabbed a warm sweater and her sun hat and arrived at the dogs' cave just as the first sunbeams lit up the soft ripples of the river.

The dogs stretched and greeted Molly wagging their tails.

Molly smiled. *It's all taken care of. Are you ready to go to Rock Lake and find the Cat?*

Rusty ran in circles. *I'm ready! I'm ready! No cat is too mean for me.*

At mid-day they came to a grove of pink-blossomed apple trees. Molly unpacked the picnic lunch. As they finished eating, Molly said, *I'm glad we haven't met any people.*

They might call the dogcatcher, Tony said.

Or the police, Molly worried.

Just then they heard voices.

"Let's have our picnic over here, Dad."

Molly saw a mom, a dad, and two kids coming up over the hill. She slung the knapsack over her shoulder.

Act casual, but walk fast, Molly warned the dogs, her heart thumping.

The little girl ran ahead of her family. "Mom, look at the sweet puppy."

Rusty stopped in his tracks, wagged his tail and cocked his head to look cute for his admirer.

Rusty, come! Molly ordered as she and Tony hurried away.

But Rusty didn't move as the girl reached out ready to throw her arms around him.

CHAPTER 5

MILK FOR BREAKFAST

"Susan, stop!" the mother ordered. "Never touch a strange dog. They could bite. They could have rabies. Get back here right now!"

I don't have rabies, Rusty muttered, as the girl ran back to her mother.

Molly and Tony, just beyond the cottonwood trees, knew they could still be seen.

Rusty, heel! Now! Molly commanded. She waved at the family as Rusty ran to catch up with them. Quickly they moved out of sight.

When they were sure no one had followed them, they stopped.

Rusty, you could have ruined everything. Molly was close to tears.

Tony looked sternly at Rusty who sat down and hung his head. *We have to stay away from strangers. Even if Molly got away, we could get caught by the dogcatcher.*

They walked along the river all day, staying in the dappled shade of the leafy trees. A green dragonfly danced ahead of them. The sunlight bounced off its lacy wings, as it captured mosquitoes in mid-air. The memory of the close call faded, and Molly felt better.

When the sun was getting low in the sky, Tony said, *We're almost to Rock Lake. See the grain elevators?*

Molly nodded, looking at the tall structures in the distance. *It will be dark soon. We need to find a place to stay for the night. Where did you sleep when you walked from Rock Lake?*

Rusty trotted up beside Molly. *We slept in barns. Hay is soft and it smells good. Cows are nice. They might give you milk for breakfast.*

Tony spotted a tall red barn with a rooster weather vane on the top not far away. *Let's try that one.*

No people were in sight. The three friends stepped inside, greeted by warm, fragrant air. In the dim light they saw a black and white cow licking her spotted calf.

Hello, Tony said. *We're looking for a place to spend the night. Would you mind sharing your barn with us?*

Not at all, the cow answered.

Rusty ran up. *Hi Cow! What's your name? Do you ever give milk to cute little dogs?*

The cow lowered her head to look at Rusty. *My name is Lucille. This is my calf Clover. And yes, Cute Little Dog, I have milk to share.*

The next morning Molly squirted the cow's milk into her thermos and poured some into a bucket for Tony. Rusty drank his just like the calf did. *You remind me of my mom,* he told Lucille, creamy droplets running down his chin. *Thanks for breakfast!*

The sky, pink with layered clouds, announced the sunrise. They came to an overpass where a freight train blasted its whistle as it entered the city limits of Rock Lake.

Rusty raced by. *A cat! A cat! I'll chase her up a tree! She won't get away from me!*

No Rusty, Stop! Molly called.

Tony and Molly ran after him. At a ditch lined with willow trees and spreading wild rose bushes they stopped and looked in all directions.

I hope he didn't run where people can catch him.

Just then, they heard panting, and Rusty was beside them.

The cat got away. Maybe she climbed a tree.

Rusty, don't you remember? We told you NOT to chase anything!

Rusty hung his head and put his tail between his legs.

Besides, Tony added, *that cat might have been able to help us.*

I'm sorry. Maybe we can find her. If I see her again, I won't chase her. I promise.

What did she look like? Tony asked.

Pretty. White and brown and gold all mixed together.

Sounds like a calico, Molly said. *All right, walk calmly and keep your eyes open for a calico cat.*

No chasing, no chasing, Rusty began repeating to himself.

Tony, I think I see her. Rusty, stop right here and STAY! Do you understand? We'll go on ahead.

Molly spotted the calico cat crouching in the tall grass under a rose bush.

Excuse me, she sent her thought up ahead so the cat would not run away. *Could I please talk to you?*

The cat sat up tall. *My gracious! You speak my language! Ain't never had this happen before. Who are you?*

Molly sat down beside the cat. The sweet fragrance of the wild roses surrounded them. *My name is Molly. This is my friend, Tony. I hope you can help us.*

Ain't this something? A people girl askin' old Cindy Lou for help. Reckon you part cat, Girl?

I don't think so, Molly answered with a smile.

Just kidding, Sugar.

Before I tell you my story, I have to apologize for my other friend who chased you a while ago. He won't do it again. Is it okay if he joins us?

That little red one? Girl, I almost had to spit in his face.

That's him, but he's promised to be good.

Well Baby, if he's your friend, it's okay, Cindy Lou agreed as Molly called for Rusty.

The dogs lay down in the deep grass. Cindy Lou licked her paw, then stared at Molly with lantern eyes, as Molly began.

We're looking for a mean cat and we heard there are mean cats in Rock Lake.

Cindy Lou stood up, flicked her tail and sat down again. *Why y'all be wantin' a mean cat?*

I'll start at the beginning. Molly told Cindy Lou the story.

A cat that steals tongues! Cindy Lou flicked her ears. *Mm-mm-mm. If that don't beat all! God only knows where you'd find a cat like that.*

She gave her head a quick shake. *God only knows. That's right. You need to ask God, or since you're in a hurry, and God's answers can take awhile, ask the thing closest to God.*

Tony cocked his head. *What would that be?*

Someone just come from God, of course. You need to be there the very second they cross from that world to this.

I don't understand what you mean, Cindy Lou.

The cat twitched her whiskers. *Child, I'm talking about a baby, a baby just being born. My friend Sadie, in the hayloft of that old barn yonder, is going to have kittens any minute. If you make it in time, you'll get an answer to your question.*

CHAPTER 6

SURPRISING NEWS

Behave yo'self, Little Red! Hear! Cindy Lou called, as Molly and the dogs ran to the barn. A rickety ladder led to the hayloft.

Molly climbed up as Rusty and Tony watched from below. At the top of the steps she heard tiny voices, the mews of just-born kittens.

Inside Sadie, a gray tiger-striped cat, lay licking the wet newborns.

I'm a friend of Cindy Lou's, Molly said. *May I please ask your newest baby a question.*

Come closer, Sadie invited. *These four have been here a few minutes. I'm not sure who's the newest, but it's probably too late. They forget the other world so fast.*

Molly knelt down by the kittens. One was white with gray stripes, two were gold, and one was smoky gray. They were squirming around, trying to get milk from their mother. Molly thought the gray one looked the smallest. *Little Kitten, straight from God, may I ask you a question?*

But the gray kitten only said, *I'm hungry. I'm hungry.*

The gold kittens pushed each other saying, *Move over. I want some milk, too.*

Sadie gave a moan. *Another one's coming. Ask your question fast.*

As the pure white kitten took its first breath of life, Molly bent close and asked, *Where can I find the Cat who stole my tongue?*

The cat you are looking for is big and tough, the kitten answered. *Almost as big as a cocker spaniel. It's in a dump grounds. But you're making a mistake . . . . . .*

Molly didn't want to waste time arguing with the kitten. *It's not a mistake,* she interrupted. *Please tell me where to find the dump grounds.*

The kitten spoke softly.

Oh, no! Molly gasped. She couldn't believe what she heard. *Are you sure?*

But the kitten no longer looked at her. It wiggled toward the others, saying *I'm hungry, move over.*

Molly met Tony who stood at the bottom of the stairs. Rusty bounded up from behind the barn.

Do I get to chase the mean Cat? Do I? Do I?

Molly sighed. *The little kitten knew about the Cat. She said he's almost as big as you, Rusty.*

Yikes! Rusty stretched flat and put his nose between his paws.

He's very tough. He lives in a dump grounds.

A Dump Grounds Cat, Rusty lifted his head. *Is that like a Junkyard Dog?*

Yes, Tony answered. *Very much the same. Is that why you look worried?*

No, it's not that. It's the location of the dump grounds.

Tell us, Molly, Tony said gently, as Rusty stood up and gave her face three quick licks.

It's back, … it's back in …in .. . Cando.

Both dogs sat down in surprise.

We came to Rock Lake for nothing? Rusty asked.

Molly nodded. *But it's okay. I've been to the dump grounds.*

We have, too. We find food there sometimes.

"Hey kid, what are you doing here?" A farmer in overalls carrying a pitchfork came around the side of the barn.

Molly and the dogs began to run. The man came after them, running fast, so close that Molly could hear him panting.

"Stop, Get back here. I saw you. You were in my hayloft."

Keep running, Rusty said. *I'll meet you at the river. Don't worry. I'll pretend he's a cat.*

Rusty flew at the man, jerked the cuff of his pants, ran a few feet away and stopped.

They could hear the man yelling as they ran.

"What the? Hey, stop that!"

Rusty charged again, then ran around the man, making him turn in circles.

"Get away from me, you little red monster," the man hollered, taking swipes at Rusty with the pitchfork.

Missed again. Nanny Nanny Boo Boo. Too bad you can't understand dog talk.

Molly and Tony had reached the bank of the river.

Molly covered her eyes with her hands. *Tony, I can't look.*

He's OK. He does this with cats all the time. The man doesn't have a tree to climb, so it's taking a little longer. You don't have to look. I'll tell you what's happening. Rusty's circling again. The man's getting dizzy. He's losing his balance. He dropped the pitchfork. He fell over. Here comes Rusty!

He might get up. We better keep running, Rusty panted.

They ran until they collapsed in a patch of white clover.

Tony looked behind them for a huffing and puffing farmer, but no one was in sight.

Molly pulled Rusty onto her lap and kissed his curly head. *You're my hero. You know what else? I'm ready to meet that Dump Grounds Cat and get my tongue back. Let's go!*

Rusty scampered ahead as they walked along the river. *Uncle and I go to the dump grounds,* Molly said. *One time we found a box of old phonograph records. We took them home and played them. I liked the one called "In The Mood." We never told Aunt where we got them.*

As gold, cream and purple rays flooded the western sky, Molly and the dogs sat down and finished off the last of the food in the knapsack.

Rusty looked in all directions. No barn around here.

Never mind, this will do. Molly spread her sweater on the grass inside a circle of red dogwood bushes. They cuddled close together to stay warm. The chirping of the crickets soon blended with the snores of the sleeping dogs.

But Molly couldn't fall asleep. Little Kitten said it was a mistake to look for the Cat. Molly had heard of mean cats that could scratch a dog's eyes out, that would jump on a dog's back and ride it to a heart-splitting final run. How could she place her dear friends in such danger? She would have to face the Cat alone. She must do it. She could do it.

Molly closed her eyes, feeling strong and determined, when a voice so clear it could have been beside her said, *Help us. Please help us!*

Molly sent her thoughts: *I want to help you, but who are you? Where are you?*

We don't know. We're in cages. Please hurry.

CHAPTER 7

SHOWDOWN AT THE DUMP GROUNDS

The next morning Molly told Tony about the voices. *I keep hearing calls for help. What could it be? Have you heard them?*

No, I haven't. Molly, I've never known a human that can understand animals as well as you can. It's a special gift and a responsibility. Some animals somewhere are in trouble and it's your job to help them.

After a breakfast of gooseberries and wild strawberries they headed toward the dump grounds. They could smell it before they saw it.

Phew, Rusty said. *This is nasty! I like it!*

Molly lifted the heavy latch on the iron gate at the entrance. *I need to meet the Cat by myself. Wait for me here.*

The dogs sat down outside the fence as Molly entered leaving the gate unlatched behind her. She felt brave, but she didn't rule out having to make a quick getaway.

Bite his tail for me! Rusty barked.

Molly walked by a faded velvet sofa with two bedsprings leaning against it, a brass lamp without a lampshade, some Venetian blinds with tangled cords and a box of *Country Gentleman* magazines.

Some of the things left here might be used by someone else. She remembered Uncle saying, "One man's trash is another man's treasure." She passed a sled with one runner missing, worn-out shoes and chipped Ball canning jars. A one-armed Kewpie doll with a cracked face stared up from a patch of pigweed.

The stench of dead fish and rotten eggs made Molly pinch her nose shut with her fingers.

Suddenly a sardine can flew through the air. Molly ducked as it clattered behind her. When she turned around, there stood THE CAT!

Molly had never seen a cat so big! White tiger stripes and white paws accented his golden fur. The tips of his ears looked chewed off, his whiskers were broken and one eye was swollen shut.

Molly knew he must be a fierce fighter. She held her breath as the Cat took a step forward, and spoke. *Yo, Molly! Sorry about duh sardine can. I was aimin' at old Growly Gus over there.* Molly looked past a heap of newspapers and saw a gray cat slinking away.

Dat chump never seems to get it dat dis is MY turf. But don't pay dat no never mind. We got more important stuff to hash over. He stood up on his hind legs looking toward the gate. *You brought your little buddies with you. Hey, youse guys! Tony! Rusty! C'mon over.*

Tony and Rusty stood up when the Cat called their names. Tony pushed the gate open with his nose and they trotted along with Rusty making frequent stops to sniff.

Molly's fears from the night before rushed through her mind and she wondered if the Cat planned to hurt the dogs.

They sat down behind her, but the cat, in spite of his tough appearance, was . . .friendly.

Rusty fanned his tail back and forth so fast it made a pattern in the dirt. *Nice place you got here.* Rusty did not want to chase this cat.

How did you know our names? Molly asked the Cat.

The Cat purred a low throaty pleased-with-himself growl. *Hey, I got my sources.* Molly waited for him to explain.

Little Kitten-Straight-From-God told me all about you. I knew youse guys would show up one of these days. Call it Cat-telepathy. He gave a mock one-two punch in the air to congratulate himself.

Then you know why I've come.

The Cat licked a paw, listening.

Molly stepped forward and looked the Cat in the eye. *I want my tongue back!*

Yo, Molly! Take it easy! He took a step backward. *I ain't got your tongue. I never had it. Little Kitten tried to tell you dat but you didn't let her finish. I've been wrongly accused for years. Some punk started dat tongue-stealing story, and dem other chumps spread it around.* He shook his head and a sardine bone fell from his bent whisker. *I get no respect.*

So that's what the kitten meant when she said I was making a mistake. I thought she meant it was a mistake for me to look for you. But if you don't have my tongue, who does?

The Cat paused. *Molly, I gotta set you straight, since I see you don't get it. I've been a fighter all my nine lives. I busted heads and got my head busted. I seen chewed-off ears and broke tails and ripped fur. Hey, if dere was such a thing as tongue-stealing, I'd know about it. Dere ain't no such thing, Molly. You can speak any time you feel like it.*

Any time I feel like it? Molly repeated. *But I have wanted to speak lots of times. I can never answer when people talk to me. I try, but I feel scared inside and no words come out.*

Dat sounds like a people thing. I never lived 'round people much. The Cat looked at the dogs. *Can youse guys help her out on dis one?*

Tony stood up. *I'm beginning to understand. When animals feel afraid, we run away or we hide.*

Or fight, the Cat added.

But when people feel afraid, sometimes they just stay quiet. You thought your fear came from something outside. He looked at the Cat.

The cat shook his head, *I told youse guys, I'm innocent.*

Tony stepped closer to Molly. *Your fear is on the inside. You have the power to end it forever. That fear can't match the courage inside you. You can talk. Just do it.*

Yo, Tony, you're one smart cookie! Molly, he's got it right. You can do it. Be brave. Be a champ.

Molly looked down, thinking over what they said. It made sense.

Rusty ran up to her. *I think they're right. I'll ask you a question and you answer it. Hello, Little Girl, what's your name?*

My name is. . . Molly began.

Tony interrupted. *Not that kind of talk. Use your mouth, your tongue, your voice!*

My, I mean "My," she said aloud.

"name," she continued.

She took a deep breath – "is—Molly! I did it! I really did it!"

Rusty jumped up with his paws on Molly's chest and licked her face over and over. Tony circled around them wagging his tail.

Molly turned to the Cat, "Thank you!" She wanted to hug him, but he backed away. She knew he wasn't used to people.

He swung his raggedy tail. *By the way, all of youse need to quit calling me The Cat Who Stole Your Tongue. I got a name, ya know.*

"I'm sorry for calling you that. What's your real name?"

The cat looked down at the ground. *My name's Max.*

He seemed so shy and sweet that that this time Molly did hug him. "Thank you, Max! You're the best!" A rumbling sound startled Molly until she realized what it was. Max was purring.

The friends said good-bye to Max and were soon at the dogs' cave. A red-winged blackbird flew past them to its nest in the cattails.

Molly knelt down and hugged the dogs. "I've talked to Max. I've talked to you. But can I talk to Aunt? What if no words come out?"

Tony licked Molly's cheek. *Remember the courage inside you. Max looked tough, but he was nice. Maybe Aunt is like Max.*

"I hope you're right." Aunt like Max? Molly had to laugh out loud at that idea. But she'd think about it.

You can do it, Rusty said. *Don't forget—we love you.*

"I love you, too. That's fun to say out loud."

CHAPTER 8

RETURN HOME

Molly's heart began to pound as she approached the filling station. Sheriff Whipple's two-tone Chevy was parked at the gas pump. Aunt had just finished filling the tank.

She spotted Uncle in the flower garden picking weeds from around the daisies. When Aunt turned her back to collect the money from Sheriff Whipple, Molly dashed to the garden.

Uncle dropped his spade, his mouth open in surprise.

Molly caught her breath. She looked over her shoulder. Oh no! She'd never seen Aunt run before. In a flash, she was beside them.

"Molly! What? How?" Aunt wanted an answer.

Molly shrugged her shoulders. She wanted to tell them she could talk, but no words would come out.

Aunt folded her arms across her chest. "Good grief! You look like you've been sleeping in a barn. Where is that Mrs. Perkins? I'm going to give her a piece of my mind!"

Uncle stood up and put his hand on Molly's shoulder. "I haven't seen Mrs. Perkins, but Molly looks hungry.

Let's go inside and she can have some breakfast. Does that sound good, Molly?"

Molly nodded and they went into the kitchen. Leftover toast and hot cocoa never tasted so delicious.

Aunt stared hard at Molly with every bite she took. Molly felt shaky. She'd planned to tell them first thing that she had lied about Mrs. Perkins. She thought of Max's confident words and how happy she had been talking aloud to Rusty and Tony. She took a deep breath and opened her mouth, but no words came out.

Uncle could see Molly was struggling with something. His eyes brimmed with tears. "My brave girl!"

"Wilma," he said with authority in his voice that Molly hadn't heard before. "Molly is back and we're glad. She's safe, and that's what matters."

Aunt's face softened. She nodded, and Molly saw a slight upturn of the corner of her mouth. Could Aunt really be glad to have her back?

Brr—ring! The phone jerked Aunt out of her seat. She went to the living room to answer it, and returned, hands on her hips.

"Wherever you've been, Molly Goodwin, you've missed a lot of excitement around here. We've got big trouble in Cando. Dr. Wellman has called a meeting for 2:00. Get cleaned up and you can come with us."

After her bath, Molly opened her closet door. A yellow sundress hung from a hanger, the price tag dangling from it. It couldn't be hers. She'd never had anything but second-hand clothes her whole life.

She turned to see Aunt peeking in the doorway.

Molly slid the dress from the hanger and looked questioningly at Aunt.

"Yes, yes, that's for you. Ida had a sale when you were gone. Go ahead and put it on. It's nothing special."

Molly smiled as she combed her hair and remembered what Tony had said. Maybe Aunt WAS like Max.

By the time Molly, Aunt and Uncle passed the post office, they were part of a crowd. It seemed everyone in town was hurrying to Dr. Wellman's Veterinary Clinic at the north end of Main Street.

Molly heard snatches of conversation from the jostling group.

"Last night, another one."

"No! Who this time?"

"What is the world coming to when you have to lock your doors at night?"

The crowd surged forward. Aunt stormed ahead. Rows of folding chairs filled the waiting room. Aunt sat down, put her hand on one chair and her purse on the other until Molly and Uncle joined her.

"My land!" Aunt exclaimed. Her glasses had slid down her nose and her hat was pushed sideways.

People turned their attention to the front of the room where Dr. Wellman held up his hand for quiet. Molly remembered that he'd been Tony's vet and had stitched up Rusty's injured paw.

Dr. Wellman ran his fingers through his red hair. "Ladies and gentlemen, thank you for coming. I called this meeting today because we have a problem. I'll give you the facts. If rumors get started, it only makes things worse."

Molly saw nods of agreement from people, including Aunt.

"Since last week five cats have disappeared."

Molly sat up straight. Lost cats? Could this explain the cries for help she'd been hearing?

"The first cats to disappear were Ming-Ming and Ling-Ling, Mrs. Larson's Siamese kittens. She'd left them by their litter box on the back porch when the phone rang. She ducked inside to answer, and when she came back, they were both gone."

"I heard about that," Aunt said. "I knew about this from Day One."

Molly took a deep breath. It was all beginning to make sense.

"Two days later," Dr. Wellman went on, "Jasper, Ted Keeper's old yellow tomcat, never came home."

"I know Jasper," a man next to Uncle said. "Good mouser. He even comes over to my place and catches mice."

"On Wednesday, Miss Wilson put her cat Phoebe in the car for an appointment with me. She realized she'd left her purse on the dining-room table. When she returned, Phoebe was missing."

"You said five. Who's the fifth one?"

Mrs. Gunderson stood up. "It's Snowflake. My Snowflake disappeared last night."

A murmur went through the crowd.

Mrs. Gunderson sniffed. "But this time there was a witness."

"A witness?" "What did they see?"

Mrs. Gunderson's cheeks reddened. "Uh, the witness can't talk. The witness was Shadow, my other cat. He was sleeping in the basket with Snowflake. He must have seen the catnapper."

"Too bad animals can't talk," someone said

"Right. This mystery would be solved if they could."

Molly felt a chill up her spine. Animals can talk, she thought. They can talk to me.

Mrs. Gunderson sat down with a worried face, and the crowd returned their attention to Dr. Wellman.

"I have more bad news. In the past week seven cats have disappeared from Anamoose and six from Hurdsfield."

"This is outrageous!"

"What can we do?"

"That's what I'm asking you. How can we find our cats and stop this crime?"

The room grew silent. Molly stood up.

"Where are you going?" Aunt whispered hoarsely. She yanked Molly back into her seat.

For a moment, Molly felt relieved. She wanted to go to the front of the room and tell Dr. Wellman that she

could talk to animals. But maybe the words wouldn't come out anyway. She'd just look foolish. She slid back into her chair and hung her head. Uncle put his arm around Molly's shoulders and Aunt sat back, readjusting the purse on her lap.

No! No! The cats needed her! Molly lifted her head and straightened her back. She would NOT be afraid. She stood up again, moved quickly out of Aunt's reach, and rushed to the front of the room.

Molly stopped in front of Dr. Wellman. She looked up and up, past his freckled arms, past his white jacket, and into his clear blue eyes.

Her mouth moved. Dr. Wellman leaned down close to her. The words came out. "I can help," Molly told him.

CHAPTER 9

WHY WOULD HE DO SUCH A THING?

The crowd burst into conversation. "Who's that little girl in the yellow sundress?"

"That's Wilma's niece."

"The one who can't talk?"

"Looks like she just said something to the doctor."

Dr. Wellman knelt down. "How can you help, little girl?"

Molly's voice was soft but she was able to answer the question. "My name is Molly, and I can talk to animals. Shadow can tell me what he saw."

Dr. Wellman stood up. "Ladies and gentlemen, you may go home now. But think about it and give me your ideas. I'll let you know of further developments."

Aunt elbowed her way past the exiting crowd, slung her arm around Molly's shoulders and looked Dr. Wellman in the eye.

"Molly is my niece. I demand to know what's going on here."

Dr. Wellman patted Aunt's shoulder. "Your niece might be able to help us. I'd like to talk with her for a few minutes."

"She can't talk. She can't help you."

Uncle stepped forward and separated Molly from Aunt's grasp. "Take all the time you need, Doctor. We want Molly to help if she can. We'll wait over here," Uncle said, pointing to a bench outside the clinic.

Dr. Wellman and Molly sat down on the steps. "Molly, you say you can talk to animals. Children often imagine they can understand their pets. But we don't want to get Mrs. Gunderson's hopes up unless we're really sure."

Molly took a deep breath. As she thought of the frightened cats who were depending on her, the words came out easily. "It's not pretend, Dr. Wellman. After my parents died, I couldn't talk any more. But I began to understand animals. I can hear their voices in my head and they can hear mine. The last few days I've been hearing cries for help. I didn't know what that meant, but now I think it's the kidnapped cats. They told me they're in cages. Please give me a chance, Dr. Wellman. Let me find out what Shadow saw."

"All right, young lady. I can't say I believe you, but I'll take you to the Gundersons to see Shadow."

Dr. Wellman walked over to where Aunt and Uncle waited. " I need to borrow Molly for a short time. I'll bring her home." Before Aunt could protest, Dr. Wellman whisked Molly away.

They drove in Dr. Wellman's van to a blue house with a flower garden in the front. Mrs. Gunderson came to the

door. Shadow stood beside her, arching his back against her leg.

"Bless you for coming. Shadow can show you the spot where I last saw. . ." She wiped a tear from her cheek, "… my little Snowflake."

Dr. Wellman sat down on the front step. "Go ahead, Molly."

Molly followed Shadow to the back porch where he sprang into an empty basket lined with a fuzzy black blanket.

You blend in with that blanket, Shadow. No wonder the Catnapper didn't see you.

Shadow licked his paw. *Sometimes I envy Snowflake's white fur, but last night my black fur saved me. The Catnapper grabbed Snowflake by the back of her neck and stuck her in a potato sack.*

What did the Catnapper look like?

Short. Bald. Brown trousers held up by suspenders. His truck was noisy.

What kind of truck was it?

Old. Beat up, with a picture of a sleeping person painted on the back window. I hope you can find Snowflake. I miss her.

Back in the van, Molly told Dr. Wellman what Shadow had seen.

"Molly, I didn't know if I should believe you, but you've just described someone I know. Your aunt knows him, too. She had the sheriff run him out of town last year."

Molly's eyes widened. She remembered the poster on O'Neill's barn.

Dr. Wellman continued. "He calls himself a doctor, but he's a fake. The last I heard he was in Chaseley, ten miles east of here." Dr. Wellman started the van and they sped off.

A short time later they pulled up to a white brick building with a battered truck parked outside.

Dr. Wellman tried the front door. It was locked. Molly peered through the window.

"Dr. Wellman, the room is filled with cats—cages and cages of cats!"

Blam! The back door slammed and a short bald-headed figure raced toward the truck.

"Hold it right there," Dr. Wellman commanded. "Fritz Jenkins! I can't believe you would do such a thing. Why on earth have you become a catnapper?"

Jenkins looked past Dr. Wellman and pointed his finger at Molly. "That's Wilma Goodwin's niece. It's all her aunt's fault! She ruined my reputation. I'm not a fake. I WILL discover the cure for insomnia. Right now I'm researching catnaps. When I find the secret I'll bottle it! I'll be a millionaire. We'll see what your aunt says then!"

Dr. Wellman frowned. "Give me your keys, Fritz. I'm going inside to use your phone."

Fritz shuffled his feet and frowned, but he dug in his pocket and handed over the keys.

"Molly, come with me. Tell the cats they'll be home tonight."

You came. You came. Happy voices greeted Molly. *We knew you'd save us. Thank you, Molly, thank you.*

Sheriff Whipple responded to Dr. Wellman's call and in a few minutes pulled up with Deputy Shimmelfennig beside him. After looking inside the building, Sheriff Whipple returned to Mr. Jenkins.

"I've got all the evidence I need." He snapped handcuffs on the cowering Jenkins and led him to the police car.

"Thanks, Doctor. Deputy Shimmelfennig will stay here until all the owners have retrieved their cats."

Aunt and Uncle hugged Molly as she got out of Dr. Wellman's van.

"Molly," Uncle said, "We could hear you talking to Dr. Wellman from where we were sitting. We are so proud of you."

Aunt sniffed. "That Mrs. Perkins doesn't know how to keep a child clean, but at least she was good for something."

"Oh Aunt," Molly smiled. "I need to tell you all about that."

CHAPTER 10

MOLLY SAYS YES

Dr. Wellman called a meeting at the city park the next afternoon. He invited everyone to bring their pets.

Aunt ironed Molly's yellow sundress and brought it to her. "I have to admit you Goodwins make a person proud. You rescuing the cats, and Uncle. . . She held open a copy of *Midwest Gardening*. "Here's his story right here—'Insect Helpers in Your Garden'." Molly saw a photograph of ladybugs on a peony leaf and another of the Cat-Face spider.

"That's not all," Aunt added. "They're paying him to write an article every single month."

Uncle's ears turned red. "We'd better get on our way."

The crowd was bigger than ever, but this time a mood of happy excitement replaced the anxiety of the day before. People carried lawn chairs or blankets to sit on. Some brought picnic baskets. Dogs joyfully sniffed each other. Cats rested safely in their owners' arms.

When people got settled, Dr. Wellman addressed the crowd.

"Welcome everyone. I am glad to see all of you. I'm especially glad to see Ming-Ming and Ling-Ling. And Phoebe." Miss Wilson stroked Phoebe's Angora fur. "And of course, Snowflake, whose brother Shadow was one of the heroes in this rescue." Mrs. Gunderson beamed with pride.

"I don't see Jasper."

Ted Keeper tucked his hands into the front pocket of his overalls. "Jasper couldn't come. He's in the barn, catching mice."

Dr. Wellman smiled. "I mentioned Shadow as one hero, but we have others to thank. Molly Goodwin, would you please come forward?"

Molly saw Rusty and Tony behind a picnic table.

She joined Dr. Wellman and whispered in his ear. "I have two friends who helped me speak again. None of this would have happened without them."

Dr. Wellman nodded. "Molly has two friends she'd like us to meet."

Molly motioned to Tony and Rusty. Come up here, guys.

As the dogs trotted up and sat down by Molly, Dr. Wellman recognized Rusty. "Hey, little pup, I know you. How's that hurt pad?" Rusty held up his paw for inspection.

"His name's Rusty. The other one is Tony. You used to give him his shots."

"Tony, I remember you, too. Haven't seen you in a long while.

"Ladies and gentlemen, some of you know Molly Goodwin, but I don't think you know how special she is."

"Very special. She doesn't talk," Jamie whispered to Pam.

Pam poked Jamie in the ribs. "She does now, and when this is over, I'm going to tell her I'm sorry we dumped a spider on her head."

Dr. Wellman went on. "Molly has a gift. She is able to communicate with animals."

A murmur went through the crowd. "My, my." "Think of that." "So that's how they found the cats."

"Molly tells me she could never have done it without help from these two friends." Dr. Wellman put his hand on the Lab's broad head, "This big fellow, Tony."

He bent down to pet Rusty who sat as still as a statue except for his jet-propelled wagging tail, "and this little cocker spaniel, Rusty."

"They are your dogs, aren't they, Molly?" Dr. Wellman asked.

Molly didn't know what to say. They were her friends, but were they her dogs? Before she could answer, Uncle stood up. "Yes, they are her dogs. As of today, Rusty and Tony are part of our family."

Aunt turned her head slowly, staring at Uncle with her mouth hanging open.

"It's time we had a dog or two, Wilma."

Aunt closed her mouth. Uncle smiled and patted her hand.

Dr. Wellman looked into Molly's eyes. "I hope we never again have to use your gift for something as bad as catnapping, but every day when sick or lost pets come to my office, I wish that I could talk to them. Would you be my assistant to help me understand what the animals are saying? You can work for me this summer and on weekends after school starts."

Molly stood speechless.

Say yes, Rusty and Tony said together.

Say yes, Molly. You can speak for us. You can tell him where we hurt. Say yes, say yes turned into a chant. Ming-Ming, Ling-Ling, Phoebe, Shadow, Snowflake and all the other cats and dogs that Molly hadn't met yet echoed the words over and over.

Dr. Wellman watched Molly survey the crowd. He knew she was hearing something he could not. He put his hand on her shoulder. "How about it, Molly, will you be my assistant?"

Molly felt like her body was one big smile. She clasped her hands together over her heart. "Yes, Dr. Wellman, yes!"

As the people of Cando burst into applause, the lid of a trashcan bounced off and clattered to the ground. A flash of gold fur sailed through the air and landed on the gravel road that led to the dump grounds.

But Molly heard what Max said before he left: *Yo, Molly. Way to go. You duh champ!*

THE END

.

CPSIA information can be obtained
at www.ICGtesting.com
Printed in the USA
FSOW02n0919270916
25449FS